DAWN'S EARLY LIGHT

DAWN'S EARLY LIGHT

By Paul Harris

STELLAR NOVELLAS

2017

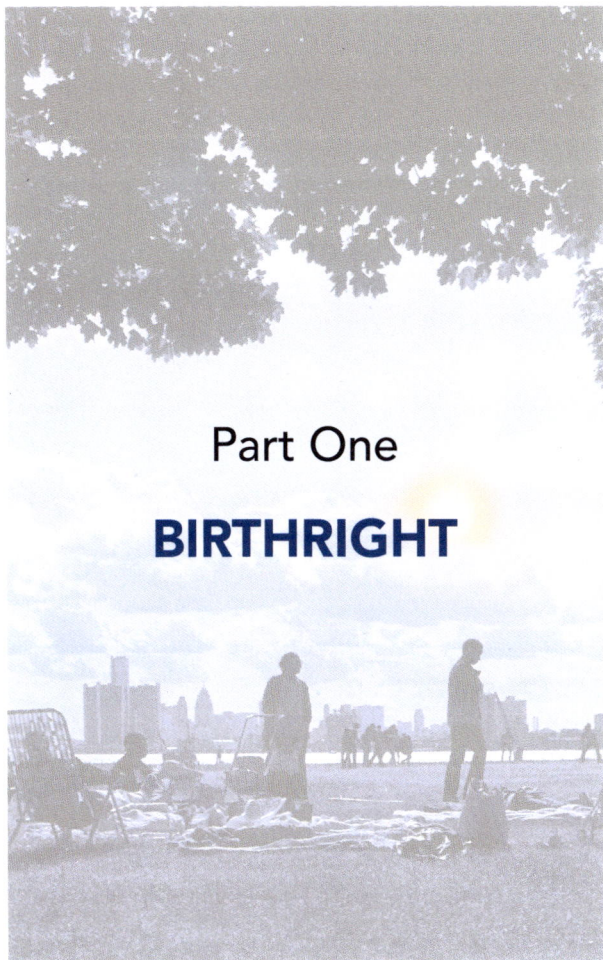

Part One

BIRTHRIGHT

WHERE I'VE BEEN AND WHAT I'VE DONE

I was born in Detroit on June 18, 1963, at what was then called Women's Hospital. It is now known as Hutzel Hospital.

I was born to Charlie and Ellen Harris. Charlie had just started work as a tractor-trailer driver with the United States Post Office while Ellen did housework for people who were well off.

Five days after I was born Charlie picked up Ellen and I left the hospital. He dropped us off at our house on Forest, a few blocks west of Mt. Elliot on the city's near east side.

He then headed west to Woodward Avenue to participate in the "Detroit Walk to Freedom" which culminated with Rev. Dr. Martin Luther King Jr.'s first "I have a Dream" speech at Cobo Arena. Charlie was one of thousands who were outside of Cobo during the speech.

Among my earliest memories is the riot in the summer of 1967 and the Detroit Tigers playing against and beating the St. Louis Cardinals in the 1968 World Series.

Growing up, I always felt apart from the other kids in the neighborhood and those who were my schoolmates. For starters, Charlie and Ellen were older parents than most back in the 1960's and 1970's. Charlie was 39 and Ellen was 35 when I was born in 1963. I was eight-and-a-half years younger than my sister, Ilar, and 17-and-a-half years younger than my stepbrother Donald from Ellen's previous marriage. I was also a de facto only child most of the time after Ilar began attending Michigan State when I was 8 or 9.

Charlie and Ellen were African Americans born in the 1920's in the South: Charlie in 1923 in Georgia and Ellen in 1927 in Alabama. Growing up in the South in the 20's, 30's and 40's certainly informed their ideas of child rearing. In those days in the South, Black children—especially boys—could disappear at any time and never be heard from again.

So they were very protective parents even in the 70's.

That was far different from the way my friends' parents—who had mostly grown up in Detroit in the 40's, 50's and early 60's—were raising them.

I spent a lot of time watching television, where I discovered hockey, or playing in our big backyard by myself.

I also always had a rebellious streak of having interests either the opposite or just different from those around me. Examples of that was my being drawn to sports like hockey instead of basketball and listening to music besides that made by black R & B and funk artists.

There was also a physical barrier between myself and most of my school friends. In 1969, when I was 6, we had moved from Forest Street to Warren, which was the next big street going north. Our new house was also about a block east of our former residence and a few houses west of Mt. Elliot.

I attended Williams Elementary School, which was located along Mt. Elliot between Forest and Gratiot for the fourth and fifth grades. It just so happened that most of my friends and schoolmates lived either on the other side of Forest and at least two or three blocks west of my house. That combined with how protective Charlie and Ellen were led to the physical gulf between my friends and me.

I was also overweight as a child and I was smart. I was usually either the smartest or one of the two or three smartest kids in my classes up through the fifth grade. That's not a good combination for fitting in.

That led to my being double promoted from the fifth to the seventh grade in 1974. That was the choice made by my parents after school officials told them that I was not being challenged and would not be if I simply moved onto the sixth grade with my classmates. Charlie and Ellen were told that I should either be double promoted or enrolled in a private suburban school such as the Liggett Schools in Grosse Pointe Woods. They chose being double promoted because

11

they did not want me traveling that long distance to go to school.

In addition to the other issues separating me from my peers now there was an age separation. Because I was born in June I was already in the youngest half of my grade level. Now a year had been added to that gap.

The result was that I began the seventh grade in junior high/middle school less than three months after I turned 11, started High School less than three months after I turned 13 and began college less than three months after I turned 17.

Those institutions were, respectively, Pelham Middle School, Cass Technical High School (in High School I was 14 in the 10th grade, 15 in the 11th grade and 16 in 12th grade as a senior) and Wayne State University. They were all located among the areas that feature new development in the present day.

Pelham Middle School (the building is still there) was located at 12th (Rosa Parks Blvd) and Mack (Martin Luther King Blvd) and was where I began going to school with a diverse racial group: kids that were Black, White, Hispanic, Arabic, etc.

At Cass Technical High School I decided that I would work in the media in some capacity. In High School I began to really listen to rock music and rock radio stations and started to actually play hockey.

At Wayne State I worked at the student radio station and student newspaper and made the connection that would lead me to the beginning of my sports journalism career. I was doing agate (statistics, box scores, etc.) at the Detroit News in 1985 at the age of 22. Just after I entered Wayne, in 1980, I began to take guitar lessons and would go on to make playing the instrument one of the focuses of my life for about the next three-and-a-half years or so.

It was also at Wayne State that I learned I had the ability to write.

During what would roughly correspond to my junior year at WSU I took a couple of writing classes and discovered that I had some kind of natural talent for putting words together.

It was due to my time at Wayne State that I got an up close look at the 1984 World Series in which the Tigers beat the San Diego Padres in five games. NBC, which televised the series that season, hired students from the student television and radio stations of various Michigan universities including WAYN-AM at WSU to work in various capacities for NBC Sports while the series was in Detroit at a rate of $75 per day. Not bad money for a college student in the mid -80's.

My job was to be at the beck and call of the network's sales clients. Pick them up from the airport and take them to the Westin Hotel in the Renaissance Center, drive them to and from the three games at Tiger Stadium (I got tickets to watch the games in between shuttling the clients) and when I wasn't doing that, hang out at the NBC Sports Suite on the 70-something floor of the Westin.

I worked for the five days the series was in Detroit, made $375 and met Joe Garagiola, Bob Costas and Tommy Lasorda.

Late the following summer I was hired at The News.

I was there two years before making a big move to the Fort Myers, FL, News-Press, a paper in a smaller market where I could get the concentrated writing and copy-editing reps that I needed as a sportswriter and sports copy-editor. The News-Press was owned by Gannett, just as was The News.

From there it was back to Detroit and the Detroit News in 1990, originally as a sports copy-editor. I wanted to write and did so when the opportunities presented themselves. I covered and wrote about a variety of sports including covering the Tigers and Major League Baseball for the 1994 season before it ended with a players strike in August.

I had also covered the Red Wings during the 1993–94 season for the first time since Wayne State when I covered them for the student radio station and student newspaper.

New Year's Eve of 1994 was my last copy-editing shift at The News. After that, I was only a sportswriter. It lasted for only six-and-a-half months because the Detroit Newspaper Strike began on June 13, 1995. I went out with the strikers—I don't cross picket lines—and ultimately, never went back.

But I did a significant work in that short period of time that would shape the next more than 20 years of my career. I was the backup Red Wings writer for the Lockout shortened 1995 NHL season. That included covering them as they advanced to the Stanley Cup Final during which the New Jersey Devils swept them in four games.

I also covered the Frozen Four and the NCAA Final Four that was held in Providence, R.I. that year.

Many of my colleagues at The News and among the other unions that were a part of our labor action were surprised that I went out and stayed out.

While I had always been an independent thinker and moved to my own beat personally, professionally it was a different story. I wanted to be successful and tried not to create a lot of controversy between my superiors and myself.

Plus, I was now 32 and since this was my second stint at The News, some of my superiors and colleagues had known me since I first walked into the paper and sports department as an inexperienced and naive 24-year-old in 1987.

But there were a couple things they didn't take into account.

One, I had had a couple of run-ins with superiors in the six months leading up to the strike in which I didn't feel I was treated fairly, partially because it seemed to me they were still treating me like that 24-year-old kid, who had made a few missteps before hitting his stride.

Two, most of my superiors were not from Detroit. They had not grown up in places where the labor movement had been such a force as it had been here.

I had watched Charlie be a part of labor unions including as a rep for the AFL-CIO—the union that represented postal employees.

Neither he nor anyone else had ever told me: "You don't cross picket lines, you don't become a scab." Nobody had to. It was just something I knew I could never do.

And I didn't.

After the strike began, I established my freelance career along with covering mostly the Red Wings for Striker entities the on-line Detroit Journal and then for the actual printed and published Detroit Sunday Journal.

Things were also going on in my personal life in the two years after the strike began. On the plus side, I had my two most significant relationships with women during this period. On the minus side, Ellen died in August of 1996 at the age of 68.

One of my freelance gigs became a steady, five days a week job, when I became the editor of the small local publication Hockey Weekly in January 1998.

From then until the economy began tanking in 2007, I made a pretty decent living working for Hockey Weekly and freelance writing. I even wrote three books.

During this time, I also rediscovered my love of the guitar.

I had sold my Fender Telecaster to a colleague at The News in 1993, when I began seriously saving the funds necessary to eventually buy my house. But I had begun to listen to music a lot more closely. So in late 2001, I bought a cheap guitar and cheap amplifier and figured I would be happy if I could regain maybe 70 percent of the skills I had developed on the instrument when I was younger.

To my surprise, in the 11 years or so that I played a lot, I far surpassed what I could do 30 years earlier. Concentrating on mostly heavy metal and rock music, I developed a skill for playing solos and played with bands in front of audiences on many occasions.

Like many guitar players, I overdosed on axes, including the Fender Telecaster that I bought back from my colleague from The News. At one point I owned eight guitars. Currently I have two: the Telecaster and an Ibanez Destroyer, both early 80's vintage.

It has been mostly a struggle financially since. The Newspaper and publishing business was already dwindling and when everything else tanked, it was like a perfect storm of personal economic tragedy for me.

I usually do all right and even did very well for a couple of years during the hockey season. But summers have been not been good for the most part.

One thing I don't take for granted in my career is covering a team like the Red Wings when I did.

They say timing is everything and my timing was perfect for chronicling one of the greatest collections of hockey talent and knowledge in the history of the game: Four Stanley Cups, six Stanley Cup Final appearances, eight conference final appearances with players like Steve Yzerman, Nicklas Lidstrom, Sergei Fedorov, Brendan Shanahan, Igor Larionov, Chris Chelios, Larry Murphy, Slava Fetisov, Dominik Hasek, Brett Hull, Luc Robitaille, Paul Coffey, Pavel Datsyuk and Henrik Zetterberg as well as coaches like Scotty Bowman and Mike Babcock.

Now, that was special.

During that time, Charlie died in early 2013 at the age of 89. I've also had to deal with lower body issues that likely stem from injuries suffered playing hockey in my 20's and 30's. This has made it difficult for me to walk.

I've seen Detroit go from immediate post riot and maximum white flight to the suburbs, to a couple of small rallies in the late 70's and early 80's and in the mid 90's after Dennis Archer replaced Coleman Young as mayor, to the most recent depths. Then, of course, to the current middle of the city boom.

Where do I think it is going? The development will continue to spread. Will it spread far enough to help the neighborhoods that need the most help? If you place a sawbuck down, my bet says you'll lose it. So make it more than a sawbuck: I haven't had dinner yet.

To be sure, Detroit is a city that has needed and still needs help on so many fronts, that anything positive—like new development, new business and an influx of fresh money—is likely an overall plus for the city. This, despite the fact that many people have been displaced already because of rising rents and property taxes, called gentrification, in the neighborhoods impacted.

Best-case scenario? That the development will continue to spread and be a boon for homeowners and business owners in enough of Detroit's outlying neighborhoods to create an overall positive effect for the entire city.

Worst-case scenario?

There ain't any, brothers and sisters.

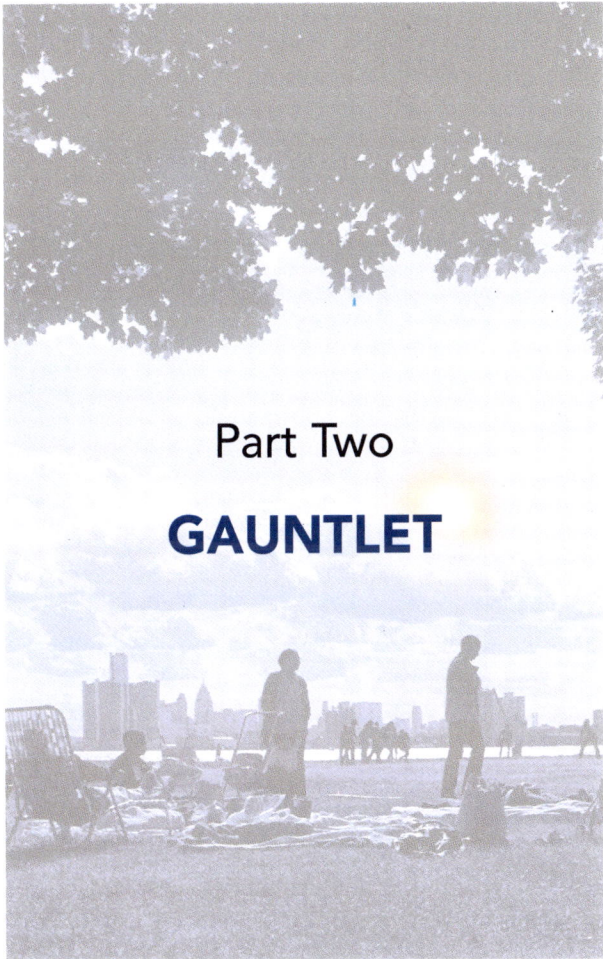

Part Two

GAUNTLET

THE BOND

Calvin

"Things sure look different than they used to around here," thought Calvin Booth as he drove through what had always been known as Detroit's "Cass Corridor".

The area north of downtown, west of Woodward, east of Trumbull and south of I-94, that which included much of the Wayne State University campus, had always been an area where many people were wary to venture into and some were even downright scared to do so.

But that was not the case in late 2016.

Most now called the area "Midtown" though a few old stalwarts like Calvin still called it "Cass Corridor".

As Calvin drove west on Alexandrine, a prime example of the changes was coming up on the right. On the corner of Second Ave., where a neighborhood grocery store had previously stood, was a leather goods store with a tee pee—yes, a tee pee—in the middle of it and where patrons were served free cappuccinos. Needless to say the store's prices were for the one percent.

Calvin always shook his head when he saw the place and did so again as he shifted his red 4-door Jeep Wrangler into neutral and made a left on Second and shifted back into third gear.

As Calvin drove south on Second and approached Selden another symbol of

"Midtown" loomed on the right. As Calvin would call it a "fine-dining foodie" type of restaurant that, while not the most expensive it was closer to that than a bargain establishment.

Calvin, more than most remembered the old days of "The Corridor".

Now 52, Calvin had grown up on Detroit's near east side, only about two-and-a-half miles east on Warren from the area that had changed so much recently. He went to high school at old Cass Technical High School, which had stood on the southwest edge of "The Cass Corridor". He then attended college at Wayne State, where he graduated with a degree in broadcasting.

Calvin was a freelance writer and a solid pro by way of his WSU credits and by bent. He could do the hard-case, investigative angle when an editor demanded it and he was equally adroit at rendering the slice-of-life gut-warmers that used to be the stock and Sunday trade of the weekend magazine supplements of the *News, Free Press* and *Times.*

At the time and many times since, Calvin had thought about how different his transition was from high school to college than was for most. Cass Tech was actually farther away from the house he had grown up in on Warren, just west of Mt. Elliot, than the campus of Wayne State. In order to get to Cass Tech Calvin took the Crosstown bus. The bus stop was just down the street from his house and across the street to either Woodward or Cass Avenue. He'd then take either the Woodward or the Dexter bus to Henry Street. To get to the WSU campus all that was necessary was to take the Crosstown to wherever the best place was to get off the bus on the campus along Warren.

When the weather was nice in the fall, spring or summer Calvin would walk the two-and-a-half miles to campus, which generally took less than 45 minutes. That was as a college student, of course.

Add that to all of the years he had hung out in the various bars of the "The Corridor" like Jumbo's, The Temple, Elmer's and many others, and Calvin had been down here in some way, shape or form for over 35 years.

Calvin was African-American, about 5'10" with a solid, muscular build of about 235 pounds. He had a flat, wide nose and smaller than usual eyes. He was clean-shaven.

As a freelance writer, Calvin had a flexible schedule and he used it to his advantage whenever possible. He felt if he did that, it made up for the financial uncertainty of the profession and its sometimes bust or boom reality of cash flow.

At the moment he was heading to meet his son, Newton, for lunch. Newton was Calvin's pride and joy though as is usually the case at this point of a father-son relationship the pair rarely agreed on anything these days.

That included how much the boom times of "Midtown" and of neighboring areas Woodbridge and Corktown and downtown actually benefitted every day, working class Detroiters who lived in the still troubled and mostly still ravaged neighborhoods of the city outside of the gentrification zone.

It was Calvin's opinion that "New Detroit" did very little to help the Detroiters who had been there all along. All those years when the city was considered a disaster area that was best known for how many people had been killed and how so much of the city could have been mistaken for any war torn town or village in Iran or Afghanistan.

But Newton, who worked for the loan company owned by the man who seemingly owned every building downtown as a computer IT guy, felt that all of Detroit was benefitting from what was happening down here.

The father and son would likely continue that debate today considering that they would be having lunch at one of those trendy places located along Michigan Avenue (the Corktown portion of the recent renaissance) that Newton frequented.

LUNCH

Father – Son

It was an Italian restaurant on the corner of Michigan and a side street, just east of Trumbull and the site of the old Tiger Stadium. Actually, Calvin had eaten here before a couple of times and really liked the food.

But that was before he learned that one of the establishment's co-owners was someone Calvin had come to not like nor respect over the years (to do with certain patrons). Despite the fact that he enjoyed the food

Calvin could not—in good conscience—continue to patronize the restaurant and put money into the pocket of an individual that he did not care for at all.

He had agreed to have lunch there with Newton only after Newton said that he would treat. As long as it wasn't Calvin's money, it was fine. Plus, getting treated to a meal by your son was an added bonus.

Calvin parked on the side street and when he strolled into the restaurant, Newton was already there and sitting at the bar.

Newton was slight and light skinned and when he got up from his chair to greet his father, it was apparent that Newton was about an inch taller than Calvin. Newton had his father's eyes but his nose was thinner and sharper, as opposed to Calvin's wide, flat nose. Newton also had a curly, floppy Afro, while

Calvin wore his hair about an inch or so long, evenly distributed across the top of his head.

Newton had also inherited Calvin's love of music and his diverse taste of it. Newton played the guitar in a rock band. Calvin had seen them a couple of times and had to admit, they weren't bad. Particularly his son who could really shred on the axe when he wanted to.

It was early fall and Calvin wore dark blue work pants, a black long-sleeved t-shirt, with a black long-sleeved button down shirt, unbuttoned, over it. He wore a pair of Timberland-style black boots. Newton, who was on his lunch break from work, wore a pair of cream-colored khakis, a white button-down shirt without a tie, the top two buttons undone, a gray t-shirt underneath, a pair of brown loafers with black socks.

"So, how's the prince of New Detroit doing these days?" Calvin asked Newton as he settled into the chair next to his son.

"I'm okay, dad," Newton chuckled. "You crazy."

"Just calling things like I see 'em," Calvin said. "Young, handsome brother with a good job and a couple of bucks frolicking in the land of gentrified, trendy Detroit."

"So what's so wrong with that if that's what I want to do?" Newton asked. "Is it so wrong to enjoy it when something good finally happens in this town? When finally, there's a reason to feel hope in this city instead of the usual old stories of people getting killed, how ghetto most of the city looks and how poor most of the city is!"

Newton raised his voice a bit near the end of that statement and a couple of other patrons at the bar turned to see what the commotion was about. Both Calvin and Newton nodded to the queried looks as if to say "no problem here."

The other patrons went back to their business and the bartender walked up. "Can I get you a drink, sir?" the young, white, male bartender with black curly hair asked Calvin. Newton was already drinking a coke. "I'll take an iced tea," Calvin said. "Can we have a couple of menus?"

The bartender handed them both menus and told Calvin, "That iced tea is coming right up."

"Thanks a lot," Calvin said as he and Newton each began to peruse the menu.

Calvin ordered buttered shrimp and a bowl of pasta, while Newton got a chopped salad and a sandwich.

"It's not that I don't think some good is coming from all of this," Calvin continued the conversation. "But it's just not benefitting most of the people and most of the city. The neighborhoods are still the same and probably even worse than they've always been. Very few native Detroiters are seeing the spoils of it. It's the people not from here who have money and the people from out of town that they are hiring to work for them. That's what I see, anyway. I won't even talk about all of the people who were living down here and were just fine but now because all of the property values and rents have skyrocketed, they got priced right out and had to find someplace else to live, if they could."

"But the improvements will eventually get to the neighborhoods," Newton said. "It's moving farther and farther out all the time. It's getting into Boston-Edison and Highland Park and even Hamtramck. It will get out to the neighborhoods eventually."

"And price most of the current residents out of the market and put in a bunch of expensive new places and maybe another Whole Foods that only the new people with money that come in will be able to afford," Calvin said.

While Whole Foods wasn't technically located in the Cass Corridor, it was close enough. It was on Mack, just east of Woodward. Of course, many consider a Whole Foods in a neighborhood to be the symbol of gentrification.

"That's the way of the world, dad," Newton said.

Calvin just shook his head and he and Newton both went back to their food.

After bidding goodbye to Newton outside the Italian restaurant, with Newton headed back to work, Calvin had some work of his own to do. As a freelance writer, Calvin had a lot of flexibility of where and when he did his work, as long as he met all of his deadlines. So, he could work anywhere there was wi-fi, electricity with reachable outlets and where he could concentrate. Luckily, Calvin had the ability to focus on whatever he was doing even if things were not necessarily quiet.

He headed to one of his regular bars, where he would drink iced tea and work. When he was done with his professional responsibilities for the day, he would have a real drink.

LUCKY'S

Marie

Calvin awoke the next morning at about 9:15. He opened his eyes and looked down to his left at her.

Marie, his ex wife and Newton's mother, was stirring a bit as her head lay on the left side of Calvin's chest.

White skinned, with reddish-blonde hair, petite and with a face and figure that did not belie the fact that she was only a year younger than Calvin, Marie was absolutely the love of his life and he the love of hers.

"So, why aren't we still married?" Calvin thought as he watched her, thinking she was still asleep.

"What are you looking at a--hole?" she said with her eyes seemingly still closed.

"Oh yeah, that's it!" he thought and chuckled out loud.

"What's so funny?" Marie asked, with her eyes still closed. "You," he answered.

She opened her eyes and looked at him. "Oh yeah?" Marie said. "You think this is funny?" she said as she reached for him under the covers.

Calvin didn't think that was funny but he had no problem with it at all . . .

"So, why aren't we still married?" he thought again, but was too preoccupied to think about it any further.

Clearly, Marie was tough. You have to be tough to be half owner of a bar—the hands on half that actually serves drinks and takes care of the place—but she was also smart, had a big heart and had been an incredible mother to Newton.

Her take on the renaissance downtown was mostly positive but for practical reasons. Even though her establishment wasn't located in any of the main sections of redevelopment, it was in southwest Detroit not far from the western Corktown area. More people had begun coming to Southwest Detroit and to her place since the boom had taken off.

Later on, Calvin—in a t-shirt and sweat pants—and Marie—now wearing a dark blue sweater, tight blue jeans and a pair of black high-heeled boots—sat at his kitchen table and ate breakfast. Calvin munched on a bagel with cream cheese and drank iced tea, while

Marie worked on a couple of pieces of wheat toast with butter and grape jelly, a few grapes and a cup of coffee.

"So how has the big boom times downtown been treating Lucky's (Marie's bar) lately?" Calvin asked, putting a snarky emphasis on "big boom times".

"You know what? You need to let that go," Marie said. "If you don't like what's going on down there that's fine. But why do you have to keep bitching about it? ... And, actually, pretty good. Every now and again we get one of those annoying 'I'm saving Detroit' type white kids who has moved here from the suburbs or one of the transplants from another city with a lot of money, who has either bought some property or started some kind of business and thinks he's better than everybody else. But other than that, mostly a lot of nice kids who are just looking to have a good time."

"Yeah, that makes sense," Calvin said. "A lot of those douche bags either don't know about Southwest or are scared to go there … Oh, speaking of down there, I had lunch with Newton yesterday."

"That's good. I talked to him last week," Marie said. "He actually surprised me by coming into Lucky's for a couple after he got off of work Thursday. How was he doing yesterday?"

"He was fine," Calvin said. "He even got me to go to Springer's Italian place by treating me."

"I'm shocked," she said.

"Hey, if Newt wants to give him money, that's his business. He's a grown man," Calvin said. "I'm certainly not going to spend my money there and see it go into his coffers. I don't care how good the food is … and it is good."

"You and your principles and pride," Marie said. "They're two of the reasons I fell for you in the first place. They can also be two of the most annoying things about you."

"You're one to talk about the same reasons to love and be annoyed by somebody," Calvin said as he grinned broadly. "Little miss feisty, smart ass! Who you first fall in love with but then have to stop yourself from choking her!"

In a little while, she headed out to begin her day. She had scheduled herself to start work at Lucky's at 2, plus she had a few things to take care of as far as business was concerned before then.

Calvin walked her out to her car, a blue late model Ford Flex that was parked in front of his comfortable brick bungalow home.

Calvin's east side neighborhood, Morningside, bordered where the blight on that side of town begins to be apparent on the west and the long established neighborhood of East English Village. The Eastern part of Morningside and East English Village were across Mack Avenue from the more affluent suburbs, the Grosse Pointes.

While the downtown developments had not had an effect on many of the city's economically challenged outlying neighborhoods it had affected this area.

Many people had been priced out of the Cass Corridor including some Wayne State students who had moved into East English Village. Back when Detroit police and firemen were required to live in the city this was where many of them lived along with Grosse Pointe Park, the least expensive of the Pointes, which also included Grosse Pointe, Grosse Pointe Farms and Grosse Pointe Shores.

Calvin walked back into his house, went into his office, sat down at his desk and turned on the old school but compact style boom box radio/cassette player that he kept on a stand next to his desk. It was tuned to Detroit's National Public Radio station, WDET-FM and a local talk show was on.

Of course the topic of discussion involved Calvin's favorite subject.

"Damn, I just can't get away from this crap," he muttered.

Calvin then turned on his desktop computer and began to prepare to do his work for the day.

THE BAND

Newton

The Detroit music scene had always been a healthy one. There were always plenty of bands no matter the genre playing around town.

The rock and punk scene was no different. Its epicenter had always been the Cass Corridor, Corktown and Hamtramck—one of two small cities, along with Highland Park that is actually located completely within

Detroit's city limits. Hamtramck was located about a mile-and-a-half southeast of the Cass Corridor.

While the Detroit rock scene was thriving, very few bands broke out to national stardom with the White Stripes being the lone exception over the past 20 years or so. Usually, the bands would have strong local followings but the members generally continued to hold down steady jobs and toured only when all the band members could get the time off or took vacations.

With the opening of new bars being part of the new development, it gave local bands—and touring bands that came through Detroit—more places to play. That was certainly a good thing for the scene.

Newton's band had been together for about five years and was called "Lust for Dare".

Newton had picked up the guitar when he was about 12 or 13, after he had seen Calvin play a guitar. Newton had taken right to it and stuck with it. He had become quite good at playing just about any style of music: blues, rock, he was especially good at playing heavy metal. He was also proficient with rhythm and blues, funk, jazz and even country.

Aside from Newton, "Lust for Dare" included vocalist Rami Howser, bass player Troy Gregor and drummer Ian Suskin.

"Lust for Dare" was a modern style rock band that blended in elements of punk and metal. Kind of a Foo Fighters meets the Stooges meets Iron Maiden.

It was Friday night and the band had a gig at one of the venues along Michigan Avenue This particular establishment was the closest to downtown and farthest east and was a bar-restaurant.

"Lust for Dare" was headlining that night, so they were not going on until midnight or so and it was only about 10:45. Newton and his three band mates checked out the band that was on before them and, of course, just generally tried to play it cool as most all musicians tend to do.

Newton favored the heavy metal look of the late 70's and early 80's—before spandex—and he wore a long sleeved black button down shirt with the top two buttons open, a blue jean vest, leather pants, a black bullet belt with silver bullets and a pair of black biker boots.

Newton's best friend in the band was Rami, the singer.

Rami didn't look like your typical singer in a rock band. He was tall—about 6'2"—and built like a solid athlete. He wore glasses, had short, blonde hair and looked a lot like Christopher Reeves. He was wearing a short-sleeved, silk, red shirt, a pair of dark blue work pants and a pair of black loafers.

Newton and Rami stood at the back of the room and watched the band, a punk outfit made up of four guys a few years younger than themselves. Rami was 28.

"They've got a lot of attitude," Newton yelled into Rami's ear over the music. "Yeah, but—apparently—not that much talent," Rami yelled back, laughing.

Rami was a bartender, whose musical tastes were just as diverse as Newton's, maybe even more diverse. Despite his youthful age Rami had an old soul and seemed a lot older when you talked to him.

Troy, the bass player, was the oldest member of the band at 34. He had played in a couple of national touring bands over the years and was the only member of the band that was married.

Troy was also a monster of a bass player. His ability on the instrument—combined with Newton's virtuoso ability on the guitar—allowed "Lust for Dare" to play more types of songs and get different sounds live than most bands with just one guitar player could.

Troy was also the only full-time musician in the band. He had two other projects: he could also play the guitar, drums and keyboards quite well and gave lessons on all of the instruments.

Troy had an open face, black hair that hung almost down to his shoulders with sideburns. He was about 5'9" with an average build. He always dressed conservatively. Tonight, he simply wore blue jeans, a black "Thin Lizzy" t-shirt and a pair of gym shoes.

Ian, the drummer, had the longest hair of the quartet. His black stringy hair was about five inches below his shoulders. Ian also had a mustache and looked more like the stereo-typical rock musician than the other three.

But, Ian, 29, was not your average rocker. He had a Masters degree in Medieval History and his most prized possession—aside from his drums—was a broad sword. On this night, he wore a Motörhead t-shirt, black jeans and gym shoes.

As the young punk band finished their set, Newton, Rami, Troy and Ian headed back-stage—where their gear was—to start setting up for "Lust for Dare's" set.

Once they had everything set up—they got some help from a couple of their buddies—they did a sound check with the establishment's sound man who stood behind a pretty-good sized soundboard. Once that was completed, each musician had a personal routine he went through to prepare himself for the show.

Newton's prep was pretty straightforward. He strolled to the bar, ordered a shot of Jack Daniels straight up. He took the glass, turned it up and drank all the whiskey in one gulp.

"Time to rock!" Newton thought.

When he and his mates hit the stage, they were all ready.

Ian took his place on the seat behind his Ludwig drum kit. Troy walked on stage with his Fender P-Bass already strapped on and plugged it into his Fender Super Bassman head, which sat atop a four-foot tall by two-and-a-half foot wide Fender speaker cabinet. Rami made his way to the microphone in front of the stage and grabbed the stand with one hand and yanked the mic off the top of it with his other hand.

Newton had left his axe on a guitar stand on stage when he got his shot. He also left one of his buddies to watch it while he was gone. This was a classic and quite special to Newton. His father had given it to Newton for his 25th birthday. It was a red, early 1980's Ibanez Destroyer. For those very familiar with Iron Maiden, in their "The Trooper" video, Adrian Smith—the guitar player on the right side of the stage if you are facing them—is playing a red Ibanez Destroyer.

Anyway, Newton called the guitar a "shred machine" because the frets are a little wider than on most guitar necks, which made it much easier for Newton's long fingers to maneuver on the neck.

It was already plugged in to Newton's Marshall DSL 100H head, which sat atop his Marshall 4 x 15 midi speaker cabinet.

"Lust for Dare" had plenty of original songs and had even put out a CD a couple of years ago but they also loved to do covers live, particularly to open their shows. Among the bands whose songs "Lust for Dare" regularly covered were Iggy Pop and the Stooges, Thin Lizzy, The Ramones, Motörhead, Iron Maiden and Guns `n´ Roses.

Tonight, they selected Motörhead's, "Killed by Death".

Newton and Troy hit the first two chords in unison. Ian did the first drum roll.

At that point, the crowd of about 45 people or so, standing in front of the stage, let out a gasp of recognition, a loud roar of approval and a couple of dudes yelled "Motörhead!"

Newton and Troy hit the next chord. Ian came in with the next drum roll and Rami did his most Lemmy like howl (Motörhead's founder and leader, vocalist and bass player Lemmy Kilmister, who died at the age of 70 late December 2015), signaling the start of the main portion of the song.

They attacked the song and ripped through it like rock and roll carnivores devouring the carcass of a felled animal: Ian, despite not having a double bass drum kit, summoning the spirit of the late Phil "the Philthy Animal" Taylor, Motörhead's most iconic drummer, Troy driving the bass and stalking the stage and engaging the audience, Rami forcing his vocal chords into Lemmy's guttural range and Newton using his Ibanez Destroyer to destroy, hammering on the instrument with his trademark intensity.

As they ended the number the crowded applauded and some yelled out "Lust for Dare! Yeah!"

The band rolled through the next few songs of the set. During their next to last song after Newton finished doing a solo he happened to look towards the back of the room.

He saw Calvin leaning against the back wall watching his son wail on the axe.

They both smirked as they made eye contact as Newton continued to play the song.

Calvin swelled with pride as he watched his boy up on stage looking like a latter day Phil Lynott. Back when Calvin first started listening to hard rock on a consistent basis in the late 70's and into the 80's, his only living black rock star icon was Lynott. Lynott was the singer, bass player and leader of the Irish rock band, Thin Lizzy. Calvin didn't even know Lynott's name back in those days but he knew that the focal point of Thin Lizzy was a Black Irishman.

He also thought: "Yeah, this *is* definitely cool. This kind of scene has been happening here for about 15 years, long before any of that new shit starting springing up down here."

For "Lust for Dare's" final song of the night they went for another cover. This time it was the classic 60's Detroit rock and punk anthem "Kick Out the Jams" by the legendary MC5.

Of course the audience roared with approval when Rami yelled the classic intro to the song: "Kick Out the Jams, mother ------!"

Newton had told Calvin the band might end the show with the song. So when Rami began to yell out the intro Calvin yelled it right with him as he raised his plastic cup being careful not to spill any of his Jack Daniels on the rocks.

The band ripped through the anthem with Newton—as Calvin noted—really letting it all hang out on the song's frenetic guitar solo.

"I done kicked 'em out!" Rami belted out the song's last words into the microphone and the rest of the band then brought it to a close.

The crowd cheered enthusiastically and a few people yelled "Lust for Dare!" as all four musicians came to the front of the stage to acknowledge and thank the audience.

Musicians are famous for attracting women and this quartet was no different. Of course, Troy was married so he was accounted for in that regard and he was not the type to fool around. Troy's wife, Laura, was at the show that night.

But the rest were single and while Ian had a steady girlfriend, neither Newton nor Rami had a girlfriend at that point in time and seemingly every eligible young woman in the building was aware of that fact. They found Newton and Rami as they walked out of the doorway that led backstage.

A group of three or four young ladies had surrounded each of the pair. Meanwhile, Calvin knowlingly, calmly surveyed things from the back of the room, looked upon the scene and grinned.

Both Newton and Rami had become accustomed to the attention of the opposite sex that being in a prominent local band usually brought. They smiled, joked and flirted with the young ladies.

Newton whipped out his cell phone, which was ringing. One of the women was calling him to give him her phone number. He looked at the phone and said, "Got it." He then touched his phone a couple of times and said, "Here's mine," as he called the number of the tall, pretty brunette who was wearing a pair of tight blue jeans, boots with thin high heels, a black, short-sleeved t-shirt tucked in, a pair of dangling silver hoop earrings.

As he began moving towards Calvin he looked at her with a flirty smile and said, "I'll definitely be in touch, Ronnie."

Newton then walked over to his father.

Calvin was chuckling and shaking his head when Newton walked up to him.

"What? What are you cackling about?" Newton asked in the annoyed tone of anyone who just realized that their parent is about to give them the business for something they would rather not talk about.

"Not bad," Calvin said as he looked at Ronnie. "What's her name?"

"I have no idea what you're talking about," Newton lied.

"Oh, come on," Calvin said. "I saw that. All the groupies come running over to you and Rami and you chat a few of 'em up and then pick one out. I saw that digits exchange."

"Her name's Ronnie," Newton said

"I'm impressed…So, when you gonna call her?" Calvin said, obviously enjoying watching Newton squirm.

"Come on, dad!" Newton said.

"Alright, alright," Calvin laughed. "I'll leave you alone ... Great show, or at least the part I saw. Looked and sounded like you were trying to channel Fred "Sonic" Smith (one of the MC5's guitarists along with Wayne Kramer and the late husband of veteran rocker Patti Smith) on the "Kick out the Jams" solo."

"Hey, you know the way I approach cover solos: Get the feel of it and let it rip," Newton said.

"Well, you definitely got the "feel" of that one! Can I buy my son a drink?" Calvin asked.

"Thanks, dad. Sure. Like you this time, Jack on the rocks," Newton said.

As they walked to the bar, Calvin verbalized his earlier thought.

"Now this has nothing to do with all the new stuff," he said. "Good gritty music in a bar with people digging it. That's been going on a long time in this town."

"Can you go 10 minutes without saying something about the new scene down here?" Newton asked.

"I was just saying how cool THIS is: People. Live, gritty, loud rock-and-roll. A little booze and a little sex appeal," Calvin said. "That time, I wasn't trying to knock the NEW DETROIT."

"Yeah, sure, Dad. Whatever you say," Newton said with a smirk.

Calvin heard his son's words and the tone sounded familiar. Cynical, with a tinge of comedic effect.

More than ever before he heard his own attitude coming out in his son's words. Calvin's chest puffed out a bit more than usual.

Like freakin' father, like son…